Tell Me Who!

ADINA COHEN

ılıı wordeee

where words connect

First Edition

ISBN: 978-1-946274-52-6 (Hardcover)
ISBN: 978-1-946274-53-3 (Softcover)
ISBN: 978-1-946274-54-0 (eBook)

Library of Congress Control Number: 2020922273

2 3 4 5 6 7 8 9 10 Hardcover

Cover Photo: Lisa Chakkalo

Cover and Illustrations: Surendra Gupta

Book Formatting: Amit Dey

Published in the United States by Wordeee 2020 Beacon, New York

Website: www.wordeee.com

Twitter: wordeeeupdates | Facebook: wordeee

Publisher's E-Mail: contact@wordeee.com

For information about the Michael Kameo Foundation, go to: www.michaelkameofoundation.org

Dedication

To Michael:

You always brought us love, light and joy just by being you.

Auntie Adina & Uncle Matthew

To Charles A. Haddad:

Who is always there to help those in need.

May *Tell Me Who!* teach our children to accept who they are and practice what they have learned from this very special story.

From his loving wife,
Joan

Foreword

On **July 16, 2018**, a very special boy was born. His name was Michael Kameo A"H and he was my nephew. He truly brought pure happiness and laughter everywhere he went. His smile was contagious and his presence so strong that he brought joy to everyone.

At twenty months, Michael suddenly and tragically passed away from a respiratory virus.

I knew how much Michael's parents loved reading to their kids…especially to Michael. They believe it is important for parents to read to their children from a young age because it encourages a life-long habit of reading and supports sound educational practices.

That's when I decided to write a children's book which would preserve Michael's memory for posterity.

There are so many traits that I admired about Michael, so I thought why not take his traits and use them in a story. I wanted all children to relate to his happiness and joy.

My message to children, and even to adults, is that no matter who you are, what you look like, or where you are from, you're amazing as long as you are true to yourself.

Writing this book has made me feel close to Michael and has brought me so much peace.

I want to thank my family, friends, and Michael's parents, Keren and Mordi, for supporting me through this process. I'd also like to thank my publisher, Wordeee and Patrice Samara for all the time she's spent with me making this book and helping me bring all of my ideas to life. Most importantly, I want to thank my husband, Matthew, for being my number one supporter. He always sees my potential and pushes me to achieve goals I never thought I could!

Do you know someone
so very small
But walks so very tall?

5

6

How about someone who smiles so big
And has legs like a twig!

Who learned to crawl
But still, sometimes falls.

Hmmm, I don't think I do
Oh, please tell me who!

Someone who
jumps up and down
And you'll never
see frown.

11

Whose hair can sometimes be a mess
Are you ready to guess?

Oh, not yet...
Oh, please tell me who!

Their eyes are so bright
They twinkle all night.

Someone who loves to eat cookies from chocolate chips to sprinkles galore!

16

And makes sounds like a lion...
a very loud ROAR!

But don't be scared to hug them
They're soft as a cloud.

Do you think you know now?

I don't think I do!

Okay,
I'll give you one more clue.

Just look in a mirror
It will tell you who...

That's right...it's you!

You can be small, tall, messy,
silly, quiet, or loud...
And we'll always be proud.

Just be... you!

Our Mission

In Memory of Michael Kameo A"H

The mission of the Michael Kameo Foundation is to spread joy and make a difference in people's lives by providing those in need during the time of celebration on the holiday of Purim. By seeing the world through the eyes of a child, we can connect with Michael and capture what it means to live in the present moment and give from the heart, which will also ensure that everyone can enjoy the holiday of Purim.

All funds will be collected throughout the year, through various events, revolving around Michael's favorite activities and will be distributed to perpetuate the festivities of Purim for those in need.

To learn more about Michael's story and to donate please go to:
www.michaelkameofoundation.org